The Room in the Tower and Other Ghost Stories

JOSEPH SHERIDAN LE FANU,
RUDYARD KIPLING and E. F. BENSON

Level 2

Retold by Carolyn Jones and Derek Strange
Series Editors: Andy Hopkins and Jocelyn Potter

Pearson Education Limited
Edinburgh Gate, Harlow,
Essex CM20 2JE, England
and Associated Companies throughout the world.

ISBN: 978-1-4058-6962-1

'The Woman in a Black Coat' from 'A Chapter in the History of a
Tyrone Family' was first published in 1838, 'Imray Came Back' from 'The
Return of Imray' was first published in 1891, and 'The Room in the Tower'
was first published in 1912
This adaptation first published by Penguin Books Ltd 1993
Published by Addison Wesley Longman Ltd and Penguin Books Ltd 1998
First published by Penguin Books Ltd 1999
This edition first published 2008

5 7 9 10 8 6 4

Text copyright © Carolyn Jones and Derek Strange 1993
Illustrations copyright © Piers Sandford 1993

The moral right of the adapters and of the illustrator has been asserted

Typeset by Graphicraft Ltd, Hong Kong
Set in 11/14pt Bembo
Printed in China
SWTC/04

Published by Pearson Education Ltd in association with
Penguin Books Ltd, both companies being subsidiaries of Pearson Plc

For a complete list of the titles available in the Penguin Readers series please write to your local
Pearson Longman office or to: Penguin Readers Marketing Department, Pearson Education,
Edinburgh Gate, Harlow, Essex CM20 2JE, England.

Contents

Introduction

I saw those dangerous eyes, the blood-red mouth, the smile . . . Mrs Stone put a cold hand on my neck and spoke.

A girl marries a rich, older man in Dublin, Ireland. She arrives at his beautiful house. A woman in black visits her in the middle of the night . . . She has a light and a knife. What does she want? And why does she have no eyes?

In the second story, Imray is a happy, friendly Englishman in India. Suddenly, he disappears. His friends look for him but they find nothing. A man moves into his house, and strange things start to happen. A friend sees a face. There are strange noises. What is happening in the house? Is Imray there?

The third story happens in England, An old woman visits a young man in his dreams. What is she trying to tell him? She is old and weak, but her eyes are dangerous. What is waiting for him when he finds her house?

Joseph Sheridan Le Fanu (1814–73) was born in Dublin, Ireland. He wrote many famous ghost stories. He wrote for newspapers when he was young. But after his wife died in 1858, he didn't want to go out of the house. He didn't want to see people. He stayed at home and wrote his best ghost stories.

Rudyard Kipling was born in India in 1865. His parents were English. He lived in India for many years. He wrote many books and short stories about its people and animals. Many of his books were for children. His most famous story is *The Jungle Book* (1894). He died in England in 1936.

Edward Frederic Benson, born 1867, was an English writer. He wrote a hundred books, and his ghost stories are famous today. He lived in the old town of Rye in the south of England, and he died there in 1940.

The Woman in the Black Coat

(*from* A Chapter in the History of a Tyrone Family *by Joseph Sheridan Le Fanu, 1838*)

I was born into a rich and important family in Tyrone, Ireland. I was the younger of two daughters and we were the only children. My sister was six years older than me, so we didn't play much together when I was young and I was only twelve years old when she got married.

I remember the day of her wedding well. Many people came, all of them laughing, singing and happy. But I felt sad when my sister left with her new husband, Mr Carew. She was always very nice to me, nicer than my mother. And so I cried when she went away to her new home in Dublin. My mother and father didn't love me – they wanted sons and were not very interested in me.

About a year after my sister got married, a letter arrived from Mr Carew. He said that my sister was ill and that she wanted to come home to Tyrone and stay with us, to be with her family. I was sad that she was ill but also very happy about her visit.

'They're leaving Dublin on Sunday,' my father told me, 'and they're arriving here on Tuesday evening.'

Tuesday came, and it was a very long day. Hour after hour came and went, and I listened all the time for my sister and her husband. Now the sky was dark and soon it was midnight, but I couldn't sleep. I listened and waited. Suddenly, at about one o'clock in the morning, I heard a noise far away. I ran out of my bedroom and down to the living-room.

'They're here! They're here!' I called to my father, and we quickly opened the front door to see better. We waited there for a few minutes and we heard the noise again, somebody crying far away in the night. But we saw nothing. There were no lights and no people there. We went outside, waiting to say hello and to help my sister with her bags. But nobody was there; nobody came. I looked at my father and he looked at me. We didn't understand.

'I know I heard a noise,' he said.

'Yes,' I answered. 'I heard it too, father, but where are they?'

We went back into the house without another word. We were suddenly afraid.

The next day a man arrived and told us that my sister was dead. On Sunday she felt very ill, on Monday she was worse and on Tuesday, at about one o'clock in the morning, she died . . . at the same time that we were outside the house, in the night, waiting for her.

♦

I never forgot that night. For the next two years I was very sad – you could say that I stopped living. I didn't want to do anything or speak to anyone. Mr Carew soon married another young woman in Dublin and I felt angry that he forgot my sister so quickly.

I was now the only child of a rich and important family, so before I was fourteen years old men started to visit our home. They wanted to meet me and, perhaps, to marry me. But I didn't like any of these men and I thought I was too young to be married.

When I was sixteen my mother took me to Dublin.

'Dublin is a big city,' she said. 'We're going to meet richer and more interesting men than the ones back home in Tyrone. We can easily find you a good husband in Dublin.'

In Dublin, I began to be happier. I met a lot of friendly people and I went dancing every evening. A lot of young men came to speak to me and asked me to dance; I liked talking to them. I

We heard a noise, somebody crying, far away in the night. But we saw nothing. There were no lights and no people there.

started to live and laugh again and I didn't think about my dead sister all the time.

But my mother was not so happy. She wanted me to find a husband quickly. One night before I went to bed she came into my room and said, 'Do you know Lord Glenfallen?'

'Oh yes,' I answered. 'He's that ugly old man from Cahergillagh.'

'He's not ugly and he's not old, Fanny,' my mother said quickly. 'He's from a very rich and important family, too, and . . . he wants to marry you. He loves you.'

'Loves me? Wants to marry me? But he's making a mistake, mother!' I said. 'I don't love him. I can't marry somebody I don't love.'

'Think about it, Fanny,' my mother answered quietly. 'He's a good man and he wants to marry you. You're a very lucky young woman.'

My mother left the room and I sat quietly for a long time. Lord Glenfallen was a nice, friendly man, I thought. I didn't love him, no, but I did like him. He always talked about interesting things. I never felt happy at home with my mother and father but I always felt better when I talked to him. The next morning when I saw my mother I said only one word: 'Yes.'

♦

Lord Glenfallen and I got married the next spring, and two days after our wedding we said goodbye to my family and left Tyrone. Three days later we arrived in Cahergillagh and I saw my husband's beautiful house for the first time. It was near a river and there were many trees and flowers in the garden. Birds sang in the trees and the sky was blue. I stood next to him and looked at it all and I felt very, very happy.

'Come, my love,' said my husband. 'You must come in and meet Martha. She cooks and cleans and knows everything about the house.' So we went into the house and I met Martha, a

'Lord Glenfallen? He's that ugly old man from Cahergillagh.'

friendly old woman with smiling blue eyes. She showed me round the house. Suddenly I felt excited to be there: it was a very happy place – women sang in the kitchen, men built fires in the living-rooms and there were dogs and cats everywhere.

'Come with me now, madam,' said Martha, 'and look at your bedroom. Then we can take up your bags and you can wash before dinner.' I followed her and soon we arrived at a big brown door.

'This is your room,' she said and she opened the door. I stood and looked, suddenly cold with fear. In front of me stood something big and black; I didn't know what it was . . . I thought it was an old coat, but without anybody inside it. I jumped back quickly, very afraid, and moved away from the door.

'Is something wrong, madam?' Martha asked me.

'Nothing. Perhaps it's nothing,' I answered quickly. 'But I thought I saw something in there. I thought I saw a big, black coat there when you opened the door.'

Martha's face went white with fear.

'What's wrong?' I asked her. 'Now you look frightened.'

'Something bad is going to happen,' she said. 'When someone sees the black coat in this house, we know that something bad is going to happen soon to the Glenfallen family. I saw the black coat when I was a child and the next morning old Lord Glenfallen died. Something bad is going to happen now, madam . . . I know it.'

We went down to have dinner. I felt unhappy and afraid, but I didn't say anything to my husband about the black coat. I wanted to forget about it and be happy again.

The next day, Lord Glenfallen and I went for a walk together to look round the house and gardens because I wanted to know my new home better.

'I like this house and all the people here,' I said. 'And I'm happy to be here with you. It's much better than Tyrone.'

I felt excited to be there: it was a very happy place — women sang in the kitchen, men built fires in the living-rooms and there were dogs and cats everywhere.

My husband was quiet for a long time. He walked with his head down, thinking. Then, suddenly, he turned to me, took my hand and said, 'Fanny, listen to me. Listen carefully. There's something I must ask you. Please, only go into the rooms in the front of the house. Never go into the rooms at the back of the building or into the little garden by the back door. Never. Do you understand me, Fanny?' His face was white and unhappy.

I understood his words, but I didn't understand why he was suddenly a different man. Here at Cahergillagh he never smiled or laughed any more. Perhaps the back of the house was dangerous, I thought. But he didn't want to talk about it any more. We went back to the house without speaking and again I tried to forget his words and to be as happy as I was before.

It was about a month later that I met the other woman for the first time. One day I wanted to go for a walk in the gardens – it was a beautiful day and I ran up to my room after lunch to get my hat and coat. But when I opened the door of my room, there was a woman sitting near the fire. She was about forty years old and she wore a black coat. Her face was white and when I looked closely I saw that her eyes were white too – she was blind.

'Madam,' I said, 'this is my room. There is a mistake.'

'Your room!' she answered. 'A mistake? No, I don't think so. I don't think there's a mistake. Where is Lord Glenfallen?'

'Down in the living-room,' I said. 'But who are you and why are you here in my room?'

'Tell Lord Glenfallen that I want him,' was all she said.

'I must tell you that I am Lady Glenfallen and I want you to leave my room now,' I said.

'Lady Glenfallen? You are not, you are not!' she cried and hit my face very hard.

I cried out for help and soon Lord Glenfallen arrived. I ran out of the room as he ran in, and I waited outside to listen at the door. I did not hear every word but I knew that Lord Glenfallen was very

When I opened the door of my room, there was a woman sitting near the fire. She was about forty years old.

angry and the blind woman was very unhappy. When he came out I asked him, 'Who is that woman and why is she in my bedroom?'

But my husband didn't answer me. Again his face was white with fear. His only words were, 'Forget her.'

♦

But I did not forget her and every day it was more and more difficult to talk to my husband. He was always quiet now, always sad and afraid; he sat for hours looking into the fire with his unhappy eyes. But I didn't know why and he didn't want to tell me.

One morning after breakfast, Lord Glenfallen suddenly said, 'I have the answer! We must go away to another country, to France or Spain perhaps. What do you think, Fanny?'

He didn't wait for my answer but left the room very quickly. I sat and thought for a long time. Why must we leave Cahergillagh? I didn't understand. And I didn't want to go too far away from my mother and father in Tyrone. They were old now and my father was sometimes ill. They didn't love me very much but I wanted to be near them.

I thought about it all day and I didn't know what to say to my husband when he arrived back in the evening and came in to dinner. I said nothing. After dinner I was very tired and I went up to my bedroom early. I wanted to have a good night's sleep and think about it all again the next day. I closed my eyes and went to sleep. But I did not sleep well because I dreamed of the black coat.

Suddenly I woke up. Everything was dark and very quiet, but somebody was at the end of my bed. There was a hand with a light, and behind the light was the blind woman. She had a knife in her other hand. I tried to get out of bed and run to the door, but she stopped me. 'If you want to live, don't move,' she said. 'Tell me one thing – did Lord Glenfallen marry you?'

'Yes, he did,' I answered. 'He married me in front of a hundred people.'

'Well, that's sad,' she said. 'Because I don't think he told you that he had a wife . . . me. I am his wife, not you, young woman. You must leave this house tomorrow, because if you stay here . . . you see this knife? I am going to kill you with it.' Then she left the room without a sound. I didn't sleep again that night.

When morning came I told my husband everything. 'Who is the blind woman?' I asked him. 'She told me last night that *she* is your wife, that I am not your wife.'

'Did you go into the rooms at the back of the house?' asked my husband angrily. 'I told you that you must never go there!'

'But I didn't,' I answered. 'I was in my bed all night. She came to me. Please tell me what is happening.'

10

Suddenly I woke up. Everything was dark and very quiet, but somebody was at the end of my bed.

My husband's face was white again and he didn't speak for a long time. Then he said, 'No, she is not my wife. You are. Don't listen to her. She doesn't know what she is saying.' And he left the room.

I ran to find Martha. I didn't like this house any more. My husband was a difficult man and I didn't understand him. Who was the blind woman? I wanted to know everything.

'Don't cry, madam.' said Martha when I found her. 'Sit down and listen to me. What I am going to tell you is not very nice. The blind woman, the woman in the black coat, is dead. You saw her ghost. She was married to your husband and she was Lady Glenfallen. Nobody knows how she died. Her bedroom was at the back of the house. Somebody saw your husband with a knife in his hand on the night she died. But did he kill her? Nobody knows. When we found her, the knife was on the floor next to her and her eyes . . . somebody cut her eyes out after she died. Perhaps he didn't want her to see his other women . . . his next wife . . . you . . .'

♦

I didn't wait to speak to my husband again. I left that day. I was too afraid to stay another minute at Cahergillagh. I knew that the blind woman was going to come back again and kill me. I said goodbye to Martha, took my bags and told my driver to take me back to Tyrone.

I am happy living here with my mother and father now. The house is quiet, I sleep well each night and they are friendlier to me than they were before. Sometimes my dead sister visits me at night, but I am never afraid. She tells me that the blind woman is trying to find me at Cahergillagh and that she wants to kill me. She is jealous of me; but she can never find me there. She must wait for the next Lady Glenfallen.

'The blind woman, the woman in the black coat, is dead. You saw her ghost. She was married to your husband and she was Lady Glenfallen.'

Imray Came Back

(*from* The Return of Imray *by Rudyard Kipling, 1891*)

One day Imray was there, in the little town in the north of India where he lived and worked, and the next day he was not. He disappeared. One day he was with his friends, having a drink at the bar, laughing with them, friendly, happy, and then the next morning he was not at his office, his house was quiet, and nobody could find him.

'Where did he go?' his friends asked each other at the bar. 'And why so suddenly? Why did he say nothing to us?'

They looked in the rivers near the town, and along the roads, but they found nothing. They telephoned all the hotels in the nearest big city, but nobody there knew anything about Imray. Days went by and Imray did not come back. His friends in the town slowly stopped talking about him at the bar and at the office; they began to forget about him. They sold his old car, his guns and all his other things, and his boss wrote a letter to Imray's mother, back in England, and told her that her son was dead. Disappeared.

Imray's house stood unlived-in and quiet for three or four long, hot summer months. The hottest weather was finished when my friend Strickland, a policeman, moved to live in it. People said that Strickland was a very strange man but I always went to see him and have dinner with him when I was in the town working for a day or two. He had one or two other friends too; he liked his guns, he liked fishing and he liked his dog – a very big dog, called Tietjens. Tietjens always went to work with Strickland and often helped him in his police work, so the people of the town were quite afraid of her. Tietjens moved into the house with Strickland and she took the room next to Strickland's, where she had her food and where she slept.

Tietjens always went to work with Strickland and often helped him in his police work, so the people of the town were quite afraid of her.

One day, some weeks after Strickland went to live in Imray's house, I arrived in the town at about five o'clock one afternoon and found that there were no rooms at the hotel, so I went round to Strickland's place. Tietjens met me at the door, showing her teeth, not moving. She knew me quite well by this time but she did not want me to go in. She waited for Strickland to come and say a friendly 'Hello' to me before she moved away. Strickland was happy to give me a room for two or three days, and I went to get my bag from my car.

It was a nice house, with a big garden. Inside, there were eight rooms, all white and clean. Strickland gave me a good room and at six o'clock his Indian servant, Bahadur Khan, brought us an early dinner.

'I must go back to the police station for an hour or two after dinner, I'm afraid. My men are questioning a man down there, and I want to know what answers they're getting,' Strickland said.

He left me at the house with a good cigar, and with Tietjens, the dog. It was a very hot, late-summer evening. Soon after the sun went down, the rain came. I sat near the window of the living-room, watched the rain and thought about my family and friends back home in England. Tietjens came and sat next to me and put her head on my leg, looking sad. The room was dark behind me and the only noise was the noise of the rain driving down out of the night sky.

Suddenly, without a sound, Strickland's servant was there, standing next to me. His coat and shirt were wet from the rain.

'Sorry, sir. There's a man here, sir. He's asking to see somebody,' the servant said.

I asked him to bring a light and I went to the front door, but when the light came, there was nobody there. When I turned, I thought I saw a face looking in through one of the windows from the garden. It disappeared quickly.

'Perhaps he went round to the back door,' I said to the servant,

I thought I saw a face looking in through one of the windows from the garden. It disappeared quickly.

so we went through the living-room and the quiet, dark kitchen to the back door. But there was nobody there. I went back to my chair and my thoughts by the window, not very happy with Strickland's servant and not very happy about the face at the window, the strange visitor in the rain. I took some sugar with me to give to Tietjens, but she was out in the garden, standing in the rain, and did not want to come inside. She looked frightened, I thought.

Some time later Strickland arrived home, very wet, and the first thing he asked was: 'Any visitors?'

I told him about the disappearing visitor in the rain. 'I thought perhaps he had something important to tell you,' I said, 'but then he ran away without giving his name.'

Strickland said nothing and his face showed nothing. He took out a cigarette and sat smoking it for a few minutes without a word.

At nine o'clock he said he was tired. I was tired too, so we got up to go to bed. Tietjens was outside in the rain, very wet. Strickland called her again and again, but she did not want to come into the house.

'She does this every evening now,' he said sadly. 'I can't understand it. She's got a good, warm room in here, but she doesn't come inside and sleep in it. She started doing this soon after we came to live in this place. Let's leave her. She can sleep out there if she wants to.' But I knew he was not happy to leave her outside in the rain.

The rain started and stopped again all night, but Tietjens stayed outside. She slept near my bedroom window and I heard her moving about. I slept very lightly and I had bad dreams. In my half-sleep I dreamt that somebody was calling to me in the night, asking me to come to them, to help them. Then I woke up, cold with fear, and found there was nobody there. Once in the night I looked out of the window and saw the big dog out there in the

Tietjens was outside in the rain, very wet. Strickland called her again and again, but she did not want to come in.

rain, with the hair on her neck and back standing up and a frightened, angry look on her face. I slept again but woke up suddenly when somebody tried to open the door of my room. They did not come in but walked on through the house. Later, I thought I heard the sound of someone crying. I ran through to Strickland's room, thinking he was ill or that he wanted my help, but he laughed at my fears and told me to go back to bed. I did not sleep again after that. I listened to the rain and waited for the first light of morning.

I stayed in the house with Strickland and his dog for two more days. Tietjens was quite happy inside the house all day, but as soon as night came she moved out into the garden and stayed there. I understood. I was very happy in the house in daytime, too, but in the evening and at night I did not like it. There was something very strange about the place. I heard the noise of feet on the floor, but there was nobody there. I heard doors open and close, I heard chairs move and I thought somebody watched me from the darkest corners of the rooms when I walked round the house.

At dinner on the third evening I talked to Strickland. 'I'm going to the hotel tomorrow – they've got a room there now. I'm very sorry but I can't stay here. It's the noises in the house, you see. I'm not getting any sleep at night and I can't work well in the day because I'm too tired.'

He listened carefully and I knew he understood. Strickland is a very understanding man. 'Stay with me for another day or two, my friend,' he said. 'Please don't go. Wait and see what happens. I know what you're talking about. I know there's something very strange about this house, and I want to know what it is. I think Tietjens knows – she doesn't like coming inside after dark . . .'

Suddenly he stopped talking, his eyes on one corner of the ceiling, above my chair.

'Well, look at that!' he said quietly.

I turned and looked up. There was the head of a very

There was the head of a very dangerous brown snake, called a 'karait' in India, looking at us with cold eyes from a small door in the corner of the ceiling.

dangerous brown snake, called a 'karait' in India. It was looking at us with its cold little eyes from a small door in that corner of the ceiling. I stood up quickly and moved away from that corner of the room – I do not like any snakes, I am afraid of them, and the 'karait' is one of the most dangerous and frightening snakes. It kills so easily and so quickly.

'Let's get it down and break its back,' I said.

'It's very hard to catch those brown snakes, you know,' Strickland answered. 'They move so fast. But let's try. Bring that light over.'

I carried the light across to the corner of the room where the snake was, watching it carefully all the time. It did not move. Strickland carried his chair over to the same corner, took one of his guns from a cupboard near the door and climbed up on the chair. But the snake saw him coming. Its head suddenly disappeared and we heard it move away across the ceiling above our heads.

'Snakes like it up there in the ceiling – it's nice and warm,' said Strickland. 'But I don't like having them there. I'm going up to catch it.'

He pushed open the small door in the ceiling and put his head and arms through. He had the gun in one hand, ready to hit the snake with it and break its back. I watched from below.

I heard Strickland say: 'I can't see that snake, but . . . Hello! What's this? There's something up here . . .' and I saw him pushing at something with the gun. 'I can't quite get it,' he said, and then suddenly: 'It's coming down! Be careful down there! Stand back!'

I jumped back. Something hit the centre of the ceiling hard from above, broke noisily through it into the room and hit the dinner table. It broke some glasses and plates on the table. There was water all over the floor. I went over with the light and looked down at the thing on the table. Strickland climbed quickly off

Something hit the centre of the ceiling hard from above, broke noisily through it into the room and hit the dinner table.

the chair and stood next to me. It was a man; a dead man.

'I think,' Strickland said slowly, 'that our friend Imray is back.'

Suddenly something moved out from under one leg of the thing on the table. It was the brown snake, the 'karait', trying to get away.

'So the snake came down with our dead friend, I see,' Strickland said and he pushed the snake off the table onto the floor, hit it with his gun and broke its back. I looked at the dying snake on the floor and said nothing.

Strickland went over to a cupboard and took out a bottle of whisky and two glasses. He gave me a drink.

'Is it Imray?' I asked.

'Yes. That's Imray,' he answered. 'And somebody killed him.'

Now we knew why there were noises round the house at night, and why Tietjens did not like sleeping inside the house. She knew that Imray was up there, dead. She knew that Imray's ghost walked through the house at night, trying to find somebody to help him.

A minute later we heard Tietjens outside. She pushed open the door with her nose and came in. She looked at the dead man on the table and sat down on the floor next to Strickland, looking up at him.

'You knew Imray was up there all the time, over our heads,' Strickland said to the dog, looking down at her. 'Somebody killed him and perhaps you know who did it, too. Dead men do not climb up into the ceilings of houses and close the ceiling door behind them. So the question is who put him there and closed the ceiling door? And who killed him? Let's think about it.'

'Let's think about it in the other room,' I said. 'Not here.'

'You're right,' said Strickland, with a smile. 'Let's go into the living-room.'

We went through to the living-room and sat there, smoking cigarettes and drinking our whisky. Strickland said nothing, but sat quietly and thought for a minute or two. His gun was on the floor next to his chair.

'So Imray is back,' he said again, slowly. 'You know, when I took this house, I took Imray's three servants, too. They stayed here to work for me. Did one of them kill him? I was not quite happy about that when I questioned them at the time Imray disappeared, you know.'

'Why not call them in, one at a time, and question them again?' I said. 'See what they have to say.'

There was a noise at the back door, from the kitchen. It was Bahadur Khan, Strickland's servant, coming in to take the dinner things away. Strickland called him and the man came into the living-room without any noise. He wore no shoes. He was a tall and strong-looking man. He stood quietly near the door and waited.

'It's a very warm night, Bahadur Khan. Do you think more rain is coming?' Strickland began.

'Yes, sir. I think it is,' the servant answered.

'When did you first start to work for me, Bahadur Khan?'

'When you came to live in this house, sir. You know that. After Mr Imray suddenly went away to Europe, sir.'

'He went away to Europe, you say? Why do you say that?'

'All the servants say he went to Europe, sir.'

'Do they? That's very strange, Bahadur Khan. I asked them before, but they didn't know. You said it to me, Bahadur Khan – but they didn't know. And Mr Imray went to Europe, you say, but he never said a word about it to his friends or to his other servants before he went. He told only *you*, Bahadur Khan. Do you not think that is strange?'

'It is strange, sir,' the man answered very quietly.

'And why do you say it? Why do you want us to think Mr Imray went to Europe?'

The tall man did not answer. He looked very frightened now;

his eyes were white in the dark. He moved nearer the door, but Strickland went on.

'But now, suddenly, Mr Imray is back again, Bahadur Khan! He's back in this house. Come and see him. He's waiting for his old servant.' Strickland took his gun off the floor and stood up quickly. He pushed the gun into Bahadur Khan's face.

'Sir!' The tall Indian moved back, very frightened now, and put up his hands.

'Go and look at the thing on the table in the next room, Bahadur Khan,' Strickland said. 'Go on. Take the light. Go and see Mr Imray. He's waiting for you.'

Slowly the man took the light and walked to the door. Strickland was behind him, pushing the gun into his back. The tall Indian stopped near the table and looked down at the dead man. His face was yellow with fear.

'You see?' asked Strickland coldly. 'Mr Imray is back.'

'I see, sir.'

'And now I know: you killed him, Bahadur Khan. Why?'

'I killed him, sir, yes. He was not a good man, sir. He put his hand on my child's head one day . . . the next day my child was very ill . . . and the next day he died. He was my oldest son, sir. Mr Imray killed my son. He was a bad man. So I killed Mr Imray in the evening of the same day when he came back from the office. Then I put him up above the ceiling and closed the door.'

Strickland turned to me. 'You hear that? He killed Imray,' he said. Then he went on: 'You were clever, Bahadur Khan, but Mr Imray came back. And now I'm taking you to the police station . . .'

'But no, sir,' Bahadur Khan said with a sad smile. 'We are not going to the police station. Look, sir.'

He moved back from the table and showed us his foot. There was the head of the brown snake, the deadly 'karait', with its teeth in his foot.

Strickland took his gun off the floor and stood up quickly. He pushed the gun into Bahadur Khan's face.

'You see, sir, I killed Mr Imray but I do not want to die at the hands of the police. So I am dying now, here. This snake is killing me.'

An hour later Bahadur Khan was dead. Strickland called some of his policemen to take the two dead men, Imray and his killer, away to the town. And the ghost of Imray did not walk at night in the house again.

That night Tietjens came back inside the house and slept happily in her room.

The Room in the Tower

by E. F. Benson, 1912

It was when I was about sixteen that I first had the dream, and this is what happened in it. I stood in front of a big red house and waited. Soon a man opened the door and said, 'Go through into the garden and have some tea.' I went through the living-room and the kitchen, and into the garden at the back of the house. There were six people there, sitting on chairs and drinking tea, but I didn't know them. Then one of the men spoke, and I saw that he was from my old school – I remembered his name, Jack Stone, but I didn't know him well. He told me that the others were his mother, father and sisters.

I didn't like it in the garden with those people. Nobody spoke to me and it was very hot. I wanted to go home. In the corner of the garden was an old tower, a very tall, thin building.

Suddenly Mrs Stone turned to me and said, 'Jack is going to show you your room now. It is in the tower.' I did not know why, but her words frightened me. I knew the tower was dangerous and I didn't want to go there. Jack stood up and I knew I had to follow him. Inside the tower, we walked up and up in the dark

and then we arrived outside my room. Jack opened the door and
... I always woke up suddenly before I went into the room.

♦

I had this dream many times. It was always the same – the garden,
the family, the tower – and I always felt very hot and frightened
when Mrs Stone said 'Jack is going to show you your room now.'
But I always followed him up and up in the dark, and when he
opened the door I always woke up. I never saw what was in the
room.

Then the people in the dream started to change. Mrs Stone
had black hair in the beginning, but after fifteen years her hair
was white and she was very old and weak. Jack got older, too, and
ill. One of his sisters went away and they told me she was
married. I didn't like these people and I didn't want to have the
same dream all the time, but it always came back to me in the
night.

Then suddenly the dream stopped for about six months. I was
very happy and I tried to forget the garden, the people and the
tower. But one night it all started again. This time, Mrs Stone
wasn't there and all the family wore black. 'Mrs Stone is dead,' I
thought. 'Perhaps Jack isn't going to take me to the tower this
time.' But suddenly Mrs Stone spoke – I couldn't see her but she
said, as before, 'Jack is going to show you your room now.' As
usual, I followed him but this time the tower was darker than
before. From a window in the tower I saw a stone in the centre of
the garden, under a tree, with these words on it: 'Remember the
bad and dangerous Julia Stone'. Again I woke up cold and afraid.

♦

In the first week of August that year I went with a friend, John
Clinton, to stay in a house in Sussex.

'Please come,' he said. 'My family are coming too and they say

There was a stone in the centre of the garden, under a tree, with these words on it: 'Remember the bad and dangerous Julia Stone'.

it's a very nice place where we can walk and swim. We can drive down together on Sunday afternoon.'

Sunday came and we had a nice afternoon driving down to Sussex in the sun. We arrived in the village where the house was at about five o'clock. We did not know where the house was, so we asked somebody. He told us it was over the river and behind some trees outside the village. John was the driver and, because it was so hot, I went to sleep as he drove.

I woke up when the car stopped, and found that I was in front of the same house as the one in my dreams, the house of the Stone family. We walked through the living-room and the kitchen and into the garden at the back. I knew, without looking, that there was a tower in the corner of the garden. It was very, very hot in the late-afternoon sun. I waited to feel ill and afraid as I always did in my dream. But the people in the garden were not unfriendly – the Clinton family talked and laughed and I liked them very much.

Then Mrs Clinton said to me, 'Jack is going to show you your room now. It is in the tower.' And my friend John stood up (his family always called him 'Jack') and I followed him up to the room. I was afraid when he opened the door because in my dream I always woke up before I saw the room. But this time I went in. Everything was very nice inside and my bags were ready for me on the bed. 'Perhaps it isn't bad here,' I thought, 'and perhaps the bad dreams are going to stop now that I am here, in the room in the tower.'

But then I saw two pictures near the bed, and that same cold fear came back. One picture was of Mrs Stone, old and with white hair, as she often was in my dream. The other picture was of Jack Stone, his face was ill and angry, as he was in my last dream before this visit. I looked at the picture of Mrs Stone for a long time – she had dangerous eyes and they followed me round the room.

One picture was of Mrs Stone, old and with white hair, as she often was in my dream.

John Clinton came back to tell me dinner was ready. 'I don't like this picture, John,' I said. 'I'm going to have bad dreams tonight if it stays in here. Can we move it outside?'

'Yes,' said John. 'Let's move it now.'

But when we tried to carry it out, it was very, very heavy. We could not carry it. We put it down on the floor. John suddenly said 'Oh look, there's blood on my hand – a small cut from this picture.' Then I saw that there was blood on my hand, too. But after we washed our hands we had no cuts, so we tried again to move the picture. I didn't want to look at Mrs Stone's face as we moved her picture through the door, but her eyes followed me again. There was a smile on her face now, but her eyes were more dangerous than before, her mouth was blood-red and the picture was heavier and heavier. We left the picture outside the door of my room.

We went down to dinner and when we finished, John and I went out into the garden to smoke. It was a very hot night, hotter than the day, and I didn't much want to go to bed.

Suddenly a dog ran across the garden and sat under the tree I could see from my bedroom window. The dog sat on the place where the stone was in my dream, and it did not move. It was frightened. It sat and looked at the tower for a minute and then ran away. Next came a cat and it did the same thing.

'Do you see those animals?' I asked John. 'Why are they so afraid?'

'I don't know,' he said.

At about midnight we said goodnight and I went to bed. It was very hot but I was tired and I thought I was ready to sleep. Without the picture of Mrs Stone in my room, I was happier and I didn't think about her dangerous smile or the cuts on our hands. I closed my eyes and slept.

I woke up suddenly; I don't know what time it was. The room was very dark and for a minute I didn't know where I was. Then, with sudden fear, I remembered. A light came on and I saw a woman, a woman I knew, the woman in the picture. I saw those dangerous eyes, the blood-red mouth, the smile . . . Mrs Stone put a cold hand on my neck and spoke.

'So, you are here in the tower, after so many years and so many dreams. Yes, I waited and waited for you, and then I stopped waiting, but at last you came. I am so happy that you came. Tonight I am going to have a good dinner . . . I am thirsty . . . I am hungry . . . I am waiting. Yes, I am so happy that you came, after all this time . . .'

Again she put her cold hand on my neck, and then her face came slowly down and her teeth started to cut into me . . . I was too weak to move. But suddenly I knew I had to get away quickly. I hit her hard in the face and at the same time I jumped out of bed and ran to the door. John Clinton was outside.

A light came on and I saw a woman, a woman I knew, the woman in the picture. I saw those dangerous eyes, the blood-red mouth, the smile . . .

'I heard a noise,' he said. 'What is it? What's wrong?' And then, 'Look! There's blood on your neck.'

'John,' I said, 'that woman in the picture we took from the room this afternoon . . . she came back. She's in there now . . . her name is Julia Stone.'

John laughed. 'You *are* having a bad dream,' he said, and walked into the room to look. But he came out very fast, as white as me, and said, 'You're right! She . . . She's there! And there's blood on the bed and on the floor.'

I don't know how I ran downstairs. My legs were weak and it was difficult to stand, but soon we were out in the garden again. We left the house the next day. About a year later I went back to the village to ask the people there if they knew anything about the owner and about Julia Stone. One very old woman knew the story. This is what she told me:

'Eight or nine years ago a woman died in that room in the tower where you stayed. Three times the village people tried to bury her at the church . . . but each time somebody saw the dead woman's ghost at night, with blood on her mouth and a dangerous smile. Then we knew that she killed people and drank their blood. We didn't want to try to bury her any more, so we took her back to the house with the tower and buried her under the tree you can see from the window of that room. There she stays, waiting quietly, sometimes for many years. But people say she visits young men in their dreams, and she brings them here. I think you know what happens to them when they arrive . . .'

ACTIVITIES

'The Woman in the Black Coat', pages 1–6

Before you read

1 Look at the Word List at the back of the book.

    a Find any new words in your dictionary.

    b Talk with a friend about these questions.

        * Do you feel ill when you see *blood*?

        * Do you think there really are *ghosts*?

        * Are you *frightened* of the dark?

        * Do you usually remember your *dreams*?

2 Read the Introduction at the front of the book. Finish these sentences.

    a The young wife's story happens in … .

    b Imray's story happens in … .

    c The old woman's house is in … .

    d … wrote a lot of books for children.

    e … is famous for his ghost stories.

    f … changed his life after his wife died.

3 Look at the pictures in the first story. Who do you think the woman in the black coat is?

While you read

4 Look at the <u>underlined</u> words. Who are the people?

    a '<u>She</u> was always very nice to me.' ....

    b '<u>they</u> wanted sons.' ....

    c '<u>They</u>'re here! They're here!' ....

    d '<u>He</u>'s not ugly and he's not old, Fanny.' ....

    e '<u>she</u> died.' ....

    f 'Come, <u>my love</u>.' ....

    g '<u>I</u> saw something in there.' ....

    h '<u>I</u> saw the black coat when I was a child.' ....

After you read

5 Answer the questions.

    a Why are Fanny's parents not interested in her?

    b How does Dublin change Fanny?

    c Why doesn't Fanny want to marry Lord Glenfallen at first?

    d What does she like about her new home?

    e Why is it always bad when somebody sees the black coat?

'The Woman in the Black Coat', pages 8–13

Before you read

6 Martha says that something bad is going to happen. What will happen, do you think? Talk to other students.

While you read

7 Are these sentences right (✓) or wrong (✗)?

    a Fanny can only go in the rooms at the back of the
       house.   .....

    b One day she sees a woman in a black coat in her
       room.   .....

    c Fanny hits the woman very hard.   .....

    d Lord Glenfallen says they must go away to America.   .....

    e When Fanny wakes up, somebody is at the end of
       her bed.   .....

    f The woman has a knife and she is looking at Fanny.   .....

    g Lord Glenfallen speaks kindly to Fanny.   .....

    h Somebody killed Lady Glenfallen and cut out her eyes.   .....

    i Fanny leaves Cahergillagh the next week.   .....

After you read

8 Work with another student. Have this conversation.

Fanny sees her husband before she leaves Cahergillagh. She asks him about the woman in the black coat.

    Student A: You are Fanny. Martha told you about the ghost. Ask
               your husband about her.

    Student B: You are Lord Glenfallen. Answer your wife's
               questions.

'Imray Came Back', pages 14–20

Before you read

9 Discuss these questions.

    a This story happens in 1900 in India. What do you know about India?

    b Imray and the policeman are English. Were there many English people in India in 1900?

While you read

10 Write the names. Who …

    a disappears? ....

    b looks for Imray? ....

    c writes to Imray's mother? ....

    d likes guns and fishing? ....

    e is big and frightening? ....

    f stays with Strickland when he is in town? ....

    g brings food to Strickland and the writer? ....

    h does the writer see through the window? ....

    i doesn't want to be in the house at night? ....

    j hears somebody at his door in the night? ....

    k wants to move to a hotel? ....

After you read

11 Read these questions. What do you think?

    a Where do you think Imray is?

    b Who do you think the face at the window is?

    c Why doesn't Tietjens want to sleep in the house?

    d Will the writer stay at the house?

'Imray Came Back', pages 22–28

Before you read

12 In the second half of the story, there is a servant, a snake and a dead man. What do you think will happen? Talk to other students.

While you read

13 Underline the mistakes. Write the right words.

   a It's easy to catch a *karait* snake.   ....

   b Strickland sees the snake in the ceiling.   ....

   c Strickland falls through the ceiling.   ....

   d The snake falls with Imray and gets away.   ....

   e The writer's dog knew Imray was up there.   ....

   f All the servants say Imray is in Europe.   ....

   g Bahadur Khan says, 'Mr Imray killed my wife.'   ....

   h At the end, Bahadur Khan runs away.   ....

After you read

14 Which words goes with which names?

   a the snake   happier at the end

   b Bahadur Khan   fast

   c Strickland   not clever enough

   d the ghost   good at his job

   Now think of words for Tietjens and the writer.

'The Room in the Tower', pages 28–31

Before you read

15 This story starts with a dream. Do you have frightening dreams sometimes? Do you have the same dream many times? Talk to other students.

While you read

16 Do these things happen in the first dream (D), on Sunday (S) or in the dream and on Sunday (DS)? Write D, S or DS.

   a The writer walks through the house to the garden.   .....

   b The people in the garden are unfriendly.   .....

   c The weather is very, very hot.   .....

   d There is a tall tower in the corner of the garden.   .....

   e A lady says, 'Jack is going to show you your room now.'   .....

   f The writer feels ill and afraid.   .....

   g He wakes up.   .....

   h He goes into the room and sees two pictures.   .....

After you read

17 Answer the questions.

    a How is Mrs Stone different after fifteen years in the dream?

    b How is Mrs Stone different when the dream comes back after six months?

18 Work with another student. Have this conversation.

    The writer and John arrive at the Stone house in John's car.

    Student A: You are the writer. Tell John about your dream. Say you don't want to go in.

    Student B: Ask the writer about the dream. Ask him to stay.

'The Room in the Tower', pages 32–35

Before you read

19 Why does Mrs Stone visit the writer in his dreams? What does she want? Talk to other students.

While you read

20 Do these things happen in the story? Write *Yes* or *No*.

    a The two men cut their hands on the picture.   .....

    b The face in the picture watches the writer.   .....

    c Animals do strange things in the garden.   .....

    d The writer sleeps in the house, but not in the tower.   .....

    e He wakes, and the woman from the picture is in the room.   .....

    f She tries to drink his blood.   .....

    g John doesn't see Mrs Stone.   .....

    h The writer never goes back to the house.   .....

After you read

21 People drink blood in other famous stories. We call these people 'vampires'. Do you know any vampire stories? Tell other students.

Writing

22 You are Fanny. You arrived at your new home in Cahergillagh last week. Write to your mother. Tell her all about the house, the garden, the river, Martha, the woman in the black coat.

23 The police come to the house at Cahergillagh. They talk to Martha. They ask about the first Lady Glenfallen. What happened? What did Martha see? Write the conversation.

24 When Imray disappears, his boss writes to Imray's mother. Write his letter.

25 Strickland writes police notes about Bahadur Khan, his son, Imray and the snake. Write his notes.

26 You are selling the Stone house. A visitor comes and looks at it. He wants to buy it. You show him the rooms, the garden and the tower. The visitor asks questions. Write the conversation.

27 A newspaper wants the writer to write the story of Julia Stone for them. It must be very short (50–100 words). Write the story.

28 Write about the bad people in the three stories. Which person is the worst and why?

29 Write a story about a ghost.

WORD LIST *with example sentences*

blind (adj) He can't see. He's *blind*.

blood (n) There was *blood* from a cut on his finger.

bury (v) When people die, we *bury* them in the ground.

ceiling (n) He sat back in his chair and looked up at the *ceiling*.

corner (n) There are chairs in all four *corners* of the room.

disappear (v) The man was there. Then suddenly he wasn't there. I mean he *disappeared*!

dream (v/n) Everybody *dreams* at night, but many people don't remember their *dreams* in the morning.

fear (n) She isn't afraid of small animals, but she has a *fear* of big animals.

frighten (v) Small animals don't *frighten* her, but she is *frightened* of dogs.

ghost (n) Do you think that the *ghosts* of dead people visit us?

Lord, Lady (n) *Lord* Binning is an important man. He and his wife, *Lady* Binning, live in a very big old house.

marry (v) He loved her and wanted to *marry* her. Now they are *married* and have two children.

must (v) We haven't got any food. We *must* buy some.

neck (n) The killer put his fingers round my *neck*.

servant (n) Rich families had live-in cooks and many other *servants*.

snake (n) *Snakes* are long thin animals without legs.

stone (n) When we put a dead person in the ground, we put a *stone* over the place and the person's name on the stone.

tower (n) The building had a tall round *tower* with a small room at the top.

wedding (n) She is going to marry him. The *wedding* is next month.

wake (v) I was asleep. Why did you *wake* me?

Moby Dick
Herman Melville

Moby Dick is the most dangerous whale in the oceans. Captain Ahab fought him and lost a leg. Now he hates Moby Dick. He wants to kill him. But can Captain Ahab and his men find the great white whale? A young sailor, Ishmael, tells the story of their exciting and dangerous trip.

Apollo 13
Dina Anastasio

It is Monday, April 13, 1970 and *Apollo 13* is flying to the Moon. Suddenly, something goes wrong. The ship is losing power and oxygen. Will the astronauts walk on the Moon? Will they get home again? *Apollo 13 is an exciting movie – and a true story!*

Pirates of the Caribbean
The Curse of the Black Pearl

Elizabeth lives on a Caribbean island, a very dangerous place. A young blacksmith is interested in her, but pirates are interested too. Where do the pirates come from and what do they want? Is there really a curse on their ship? And why can't they enjoy their gold?

There are hundreds of Penguin Readers to choose from – world classics, film adaptations, modern-day crime and adventure, short stories, biographies, American classics, non-fiction, plays ...

For a complete list of all Penguin Readers titles, please contact your local Pearson Longman office or visit our website.

www.penguinreaders.com

Longman Dictionaries

Express yourself with confidence!

Longman has led the way in ELT dictionaries since 1935. We constantly talk to students and teachers around the world to find out what they need from a learner's dictionary.

Why choose a Longman dictionary?

Easy to understand

Longman invented the Defining Vocabulary – 2000 of the most common words which are used to write the definitions in our dictionaries. So Longman definitions are always clear and easy to understand.

Real, natural English

All Longman dictionaries contain natural examples taken from real-life that help explain the meaning of a word and show you how to use it in context.

Avoid common mistakes

Longman dictionaries are written specially for learners, and we make sure that you get all the help you need to avoid common mistakes. We analyse typical learners' mistakes and include notes on how to avoid them.

Innovative CD-ROMs

Longman are leaders in dictionary CD-ROM innovation. Did you know that a dictionary CD-ROM includes features to help improve your pronunciation, help you practice for exams and improve your writing skills?

For details of all Longman dictionaries, and to choose the one that's right for you, visit our website:

www.longman.com/dictionaries